D0908490

For Michael
my Hero
♡

First published in Great Britain in 2003
by Orion Children's Books
a division of the Orion Publishing Group Ltd
Orion House
5 Upper St Martin's Lane
London WC2H 9EA

Text and illustrations © Madeleine Floyd 2003

Design by Sarah Hodder

The right of Madeleine Floyd to be identified as the author and illustrator of
this work has been asserted.

All rights reserved. No part of this publication may be reproduced, stored in a
retrieval system, or transmitted, in any form or by any means, electronic,
mechanical, photocopying, recording, or otherwise, without the prior
permission of Orion Children's Books.

A catalogue record for this book is available from the British Library.

Printed in Italy

Captain's Purr

written and illustrated by
Madeleine Floyd

Orion
Children's Books

This is our house by the river where we live.

Here is Captain, our very handsome cat.

We love Captain.

Captain likes to sleep.

He sleeps on my bed.

He sleeps on my books.

He sleeps at the top

of the stairs

and he sleeps on

the roof of the

garden shed.

When he is not sleeping, Captain likes to wash.

He washes his ears.

He washes his paws.

He washes his back

and he washes his long tail.

When he is not sleeping or washing, Captain likes to eat.

He eats cat food from small round tins.

He eats cat biscuits from large square boxes.

He eats pink salmon from his special blue plate

and if he is lucky he eats little bits of roast chicken

left over from our supper.

When he is not sleeping, washing or eating,

Captain goes out in the moonlight.

He strolls down to the river.

He jumps into his rowing boat.

He picks up the oars and he rows and he rows

until he reaches the house where his sweetheart lives.

They sit in his boat under the stars,

holding paws and smiling at each other.

Before morning comes

Captain says goodbye.

He rows back up the river,

jumps out of his rowing boat,

strolls back up the garden path,

climbs up the stairs,

springs back up on to my bed

and purrs very loudly.

When Captain is not sleeping, washing, eating, rowing

or holding paws with his sweetheart, he likes to purr.

Captain purrs

and he purrs

and he purrs

and he purrs.